"Beloved Local Teacher Becomes Newest Celebrity!"

LV NEWS

The Teacher Who Would Not Retire
Loses Her Ballet Slippers

Story by Sheila & Letty Sustrin
Illustrations by Thomas H. Boné III

Blue Marlin Publications

The Teacher Who Would Not Retire
Loses Her Ballet Slippers

Published by Blue Marlin Publications

Text copyright © 2014 by Sheila & Letty Sustrin

Illustrations copyright © 2014 by Blue Marlin Publications

First printing 2014

Library of Congress Cataloging-in-Publication Data

Sustrin, Sheila, author.
 The teacher who would not retire loses her ballet slippers / story by Sheila & Letty Sustrin; illustrations by Thomas H. Bone III.
     pages cm
 Summary: "Mrs. Belle has lost her ballet slippers, and the entire town must join forces to help her find them"-- Provided by publisher.
 ISBN 978-0-9885295-4-0
 I. Sustrin, Letty, author. II. Boné, Thomas H., illustrator III. Title.
 PZ7.S96584Tg 2014
 [E]--dc23
                          2014021168

Job #141517

Blue Marlin Publications, Ltd.
823 Aberdeen Road, West Bay Shore, NY 11706
www.bluemarlinpubs.com

Printed and bound by Regent Publishing Services Limited in China.
Book design & layout by Jude Rich

For Belle,

Our beloved Scottish Terrier who has given us much joy and love

And for

Maria Canale, Noreen LoConte, & Marie Poppo, our very own Three Musketeers

"All for one and one for all"

- LS & SS

To my wife, Shantel, and our children: Ciana, Jalena and Jaron. You are my joy and loving motivation behind every drawing I make!

- THB

Mrs. Belle looked at herself in the mirror and said, "My goodness, I look like I've gained a few pounds." Then she took one look at Kitty Belle and said, "I think BOTH of us have been eating too many goodies. Tomorrow we must start to exercise."

The next day, when Mrs. Belle and Kitty Belle came home after jogging, Mrs. Belle looked at her March Calendar and said, "Today is the first day of Spring. What a perfect time to start my Spring Cleaning."

She spent the whole morning dusting the furniture, sweeping and washing all the floors, and putting up new curtains. Then she went upstairs to her bedroom. When she opened her special ballet slipper closet, it was a MESS! Mrs. Belle said, "Oh my! I didn't realize how soiled they have gotten. I am going to clean all my slippers, and they will look like they are brand new."

Mrs. Belle put on the flippers the children had decorated for her when she was the teacher at the Laurelville Town Camp. This way, she wouldn't slip if the ground got very wet. She washed all five pairs of slippers in a great big washtub in her backyard. She used the hose to rinse off all the soap suds. Finally, she hung them on the clothesline to dry.

The next morning, the doorbell woke Mrs. Belle, and she ran down to find Mr. Rivera and Magic at the door. "Mrs. Belle, why aren't you dressed yet? Today is Friday. It's your reading day at the Laurelville School Library, and I came by to pick you up."

Mrs. Belle answered, "Oh Mr. Rivera, I'm so sorry. All the Spring Cleaning I did yesterday made me so tired that I overslept. I'll hurry and get ready."

As Mr. Rivera was putting milk into Kitty Belle's bowl, there was a loud SHRIEK coming from the backyard. They ran outside, and there was Mrs. Belle, tears running down her face, standing in front of an empty clothesline.

"Where are all my ballet slippers? They've disappeared! Call the Police! Call the Fire Department! I must find them. The children love them so."

Mr. Rivera said, "Please put on any pair of shoes for now, and I promise you that when reading time is over, we'll all help you look for the missing ballet slippers."

When the children arrived in the school library, they looked at Mrs. Belle, and giggled. She was wearing her flippers. "What happened?" they all asked. Mrs. Belle told them about the missing slippers. She had no other shoes but her flippers. All the children chanted:

Mrs. Belle, what can we do?
We must find your slippers for you.
We don't want to see you sad.
We only like to see you glad.

Suddenly, Mr. Rivera made an announcement on the Loud Speaker:

Attention! Attention! We are organizing a search
for Mrs. Belle's ballet slippers. Everyone will meet at
her house at 4:00 P.M.

There was such excitement on Mrs. Belle's street. The school buses brought the children. The townspeople came marching down the street. The policemen came riding cars, motorcycles, and horses. The fire chief rang the fire bell as he drove the fire truck.

Mr. Rivera's dog, Magic, brought all the other dogs from the neighborhood to help sniff for the scent of the ballet slippers. Even the school cook was there to serve hot dogs and ice cream in case anyone got hungry during the search.

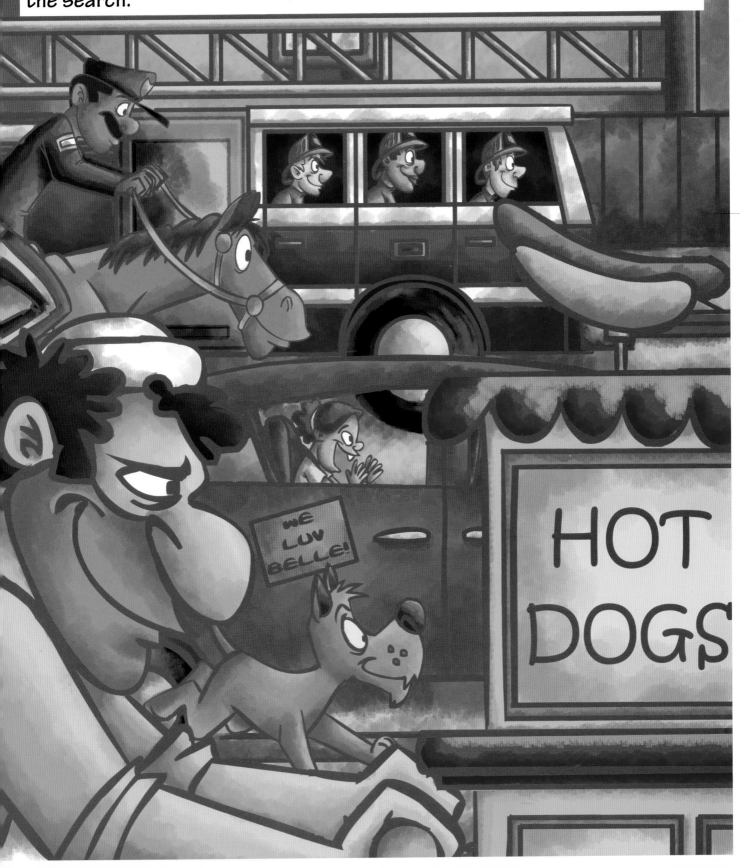

Police Chief Jaron put a huge map of Laurelville on Mrs. Belle's garage door. Mrs. Belle and all her friends listened very carefully as he explained: "I have divided our town into four sections: North, East, South, and West. We will have four groups, and each group will search one of the sections."

He turned to Mrs. Belle and said, "You will stay here, and we will call you with all the progress reports. Please record everything on the map." He gave her some red ballet stickers that said, "NO SLIPPERS."

On her driveway, ten cell phones were set up. Mrs. Belle said, "I have all the phones on and ready to use."

The four groups began to march in different directions. Mrs. Belle heard them all chanting:

Mrs. Belle, what can we do?
We must find your slippers for you.
We don't want to see you sad.
We only like to see you glad.

The cell phones kept ringing and ringing. Poor Mrs. Belle was getting so dizzy running from one phone to the other. Every time she answered one, she hoped there would be good news. She waited, and waited, and waited!

Fire Chief Henry called from the North section where the school was located. He said, "Mrs. Belle, we have searched this whole area, and I am sorry to say that your ballet slippers are not here."

Mrs. Belle tried so hard not to cry as she put a red "NO SLIPPERS" sticker on the North section of town.

The phones rang again. She picked one up, and Mr. Rivera was shouting, "Mrs. Belle, I'm in the East part of Laurelville where the town garbage dump is, and Magic and the other dogs are sniffing and barking. We can see some colorful spots in the middle of the dump. The spots might be your ballet slippers! We'll be there in a few minutes to pick you up."

Mrs. Belle got so excited and hopeful. Wouldn't it be wonderful if the mystery was solved? She heard a loud noise, and a helicopter was landing in front of her house. Mr. Rivera and Magic jumped out, ran and grabbed Mrs. Belle, and before you could count 1,2,3, they were in the helicopter and back up in the air.

When they got to the dump, the pilot let a long rope ladder drop out of the helicopter right above the colorful spots. Mrs. Belle was so brave. She went down the ladder to see if they were her slippers. As she descended, all the children sang:

Mrs. Belle, what can we do?
We must find your slippers for you.
We don't want to see you sad.
We only like to see you glad.

Mrs. Belle and Mr. Rivera landed on top of the garbage pile. Mrs. Belle shouted above the helicopter noise, "Oh no, it's not my ballet slippers. These are my old, broken umbrellas with the ballet slipper patterns. I threw them out last week." How disappointed Mrs. Belle was as they brought her back to her house. Now, she had to put a red "NO SLIPPERS" sticker on the map's East section of town.

As Mrs. Belle sat on the porch steps, Kitty Belle jumped on her lap and licked her face. "Oh Kitty Belle, what am I going to do?"

Mrs. Belle answered one of her phones. It was Police Chief Jaron. "Mrs. Belle! Mrs. Belle!," he shouted. "I'm in the South section of town and I think I've found your ballet slippers at the Laurelville Park. We see their ribbons hanging from the branches of a tree, but I need you to identify them. I'll be there in 10 minutes to pick you up."

As the police chief's horse galloped up to Mrs. Belle's house, Police Chief Jaron bent down, grabbed her, and sat her behind him. Mrs. Belle had NEVER been on a horse before. She was frightened and held on tightly. Kitty Belle was so excited to be on a horse!

When they got to the park, everyone was there. The children chanted:

Mrs. Belle, what can we do?
We must find your slippers for you.
We don't want to see you sad.
We only like to see you glad.

Mrs. Belle took one look and said, "Oh my, how did my ballet slippers get up into the tree? Get me a ladder at once."

Meanwhile, Kitty Belle quickly climbed the trunk of the tree and began pulling on the ribbons. She got all tangled up in them. Mrs. Belle raced up the ladder. She turned around, looking very sad, and said, "Oh no, it's not my ballet slippers." She reached higher and pulled out a huge kite. The colorful ribbons were from the tail of the kite.

When Mrs. Belle returned to her house, she put a "NO SLIPPERS" sticker on the South section of the map. She decided to check under all the furniture in the house, but she found only her old bedroom slippers under her bed.

Fire Chief Henry called and said, "Mrs. Belle, we're coming to check the west side of town where you live."

Back came Mr. Rivera with all the townspeople marching behind him! Back came Magic with all the dogs following him! Back came Fire Chief Henry and Police Chief Jaron!

Mr. Rivera shouted, "Everyone spread out and check every part of the area around Mrs. Belle's house."

LET THE SEARCH BEGIN!

They found colorful rocks, little pieces of colored papers that blew in the wind, and even some bright colored bugs. BUT no ballet slippers.

SUDDENLY, Mr. Mayor called out, "I see them! I see them! Mrs. Belle's slippers are at the bottom of her pool."

As Mrs. Belle ran into her house, she shouted, "I'll be right there." Then she came running towards the swimming pool dressed in her snorkeling outfit. Mrs. Belle quickly climbed to the top of the diving board and jumped into the pool. Splashing around, she announced, "Oh no, Mr. Mayor was wrong. I completely forgot that the bottom of the new liner in my swimming pool has a painted pattern of colorful ballet slippers."

All the children said:

Mrs. Belle, what can we do?
We must find your slippers for you.
We don't want to see you sad.
We only like to see you glad.

Just then, Kitty Belle jumped into Mrs. Belle's arms. "My goodness, I think Kitty Belle is trying to tell me something." Kitty Belle and Magic raced to the house, and everyone followed. The two animals led them into Mrs. Belle's bedroom and right up to the door of her ballet slipper closet.

Mrs. Belle opened the door, and there were the five pairs of ballet slippers. Mrs. Belle said, "Now I know why Kitty Belle got sooooo fat!" In each of the ten ballet slippers was a tiny, newborn kitten.

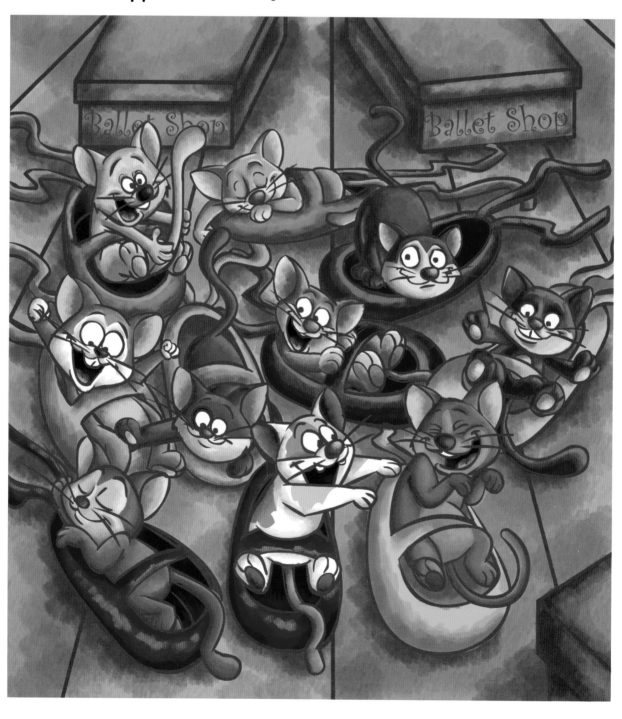

veryone was so excited. Mr. Rivera said, "Kitty Belle must have pulled the ballet ippers off the clothesline and brought them back up to the closet. Then, when e had her kittens, she put each one in a slipper."

ow that the mystery is solved, it is quiet once again at Mrs. Belle's house. Kitty elle loves being a mother, and at night, the ten little kittens curl up on their eeny-tiny pillows on Mrs. Belle's bed.

And, best of all, Mrs. Belle has her ballet slippers back!

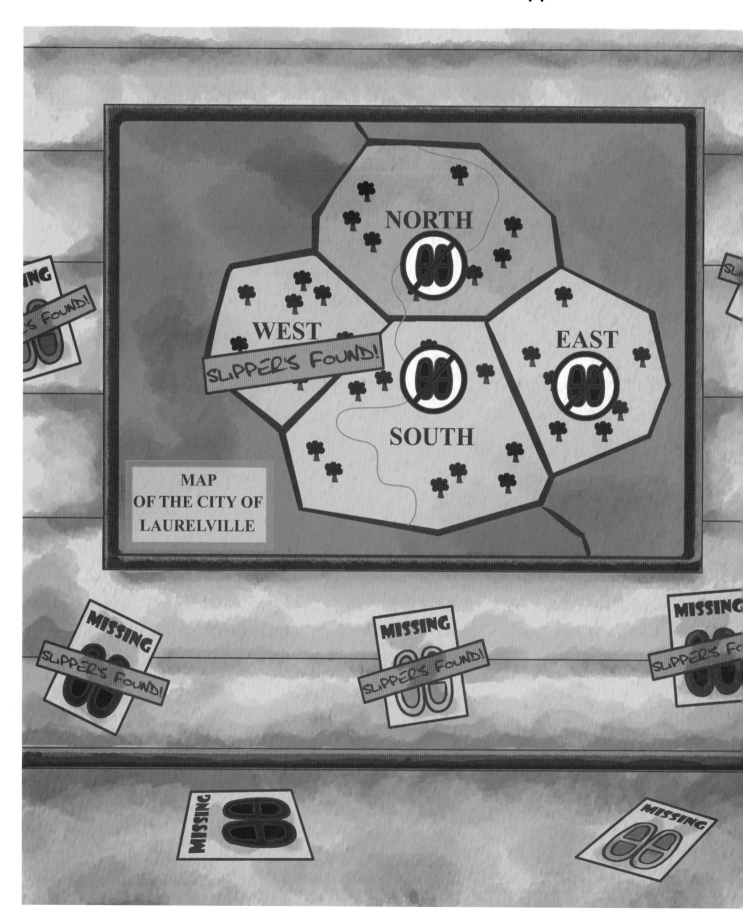